COUNTRY EXPLORERS

INDIA

Tom Streissguth

Lerner Publications Company • Minneapolis

Lerner Publications Company
A division of Lerner Publishing Group, Inc.
241 First Avenue North
Minneapolis, MN 55401 U.S.A.

Website address: www.lernerbooks.com

Library of Congress Cataloging-in-Publication Data

Streissguth, Thomas, 1958–
    India / by Tom Streissguth.
      p. cm. — (Country explorers)
    Includes index.
    ISBN-13: 978–0–8225–8662–3 (lib. bdg. : alk. paper)
    1. India—Juvenile literature. I. Title.
  DS407.S86 2008   2007019772

Manufactured in the United States of America
1 2 3 4 5 6 – JR – 13 12 11 10 09 08

Table of Contents

Welcome!

We're going to India! India lies on the continent of Asia. On a map, the country looks a little like a diamond. Pakistan, China, Nepal, Bhutan, and Bangladesh touch India's northern side. And do you see the land between Bangladesh and Myanmar? It's part of India too. It's called Assam.

Water surrounds much of India. The Arabian Sea lies to the west. The Bay of Bengal is to the east. Off the southern tip of India sits Sri Lanka. Sri Lanka is an island country. It is shaped like a teardrop.

The Arabian Sea laps the shoreline of this western Indian beach.

CHINA

PAKISTAN

NEPAL

INDUS RIVER

INDUS RIVER

India

BHUTAN

New Delhi

Agra

H I M A L A Y A

INDO-GANGETIC PLAIN

GANGES RIVER

INDIA

ASSAM

BRAHMAPUTRA RIVER

NARMADA RIVER

BANGLADESH

Kolkata

MAHANADI RIVER

MYANMAR

GODAVARI RIVER

Mumbai

DECCAN PLATEAU

KRISHNA RIVER

ARABIAN SEA

MILES
0   200   400

0   200   400   600
KILOMETERS

BAY
OF
BENGAL

CAUVERY RIVER

TAMIL NADU

mountains
plains
plateau
desert
region
country's capital

SRI LANKA

The Himalayas

Huge mountains run between India and the rest of Asia. The mountains are called the Himalayas. The Himalayas formed millions and millions of years ago.

The Himalayas soar above this city in West Bengal. West Bengal is a state in the eastern part of India.

6

At that time, India was not a part of Asia. It was a separate piece of land. But then, India and Asia began to move. They crashed into each other. The crash pushed some of the land upward toward the sky. This land became the towering Himalayas.

Snowy Mount Shivling is part of the Himalayas.

Map Whiz Quiz

Take a look at the map on page 5. A map is a drawing or chart of a place. Trace the outline of India onto a sheet of paper. See if you can find the Arabian Sea. Mark this side of your map with a *W* for west. How about the Bay of Bengal? Mark this side with an *E* for east. With a green crayon, color in India. Color Nepal, Bhutan, and Bangladesh yellow to show where they end and India begins.

Big River

Splash! Many rivers flow through India. But the most important river is the Ganges. Get this: the Ganges is 1,500 miles (2,414 kilometers) long!

The banks of the Ganges stretch on for miles.

The Ganges starts in the Himalayas. It drifts across the plains of northern India. Eventually, the river empties into the Bay of Bengal.

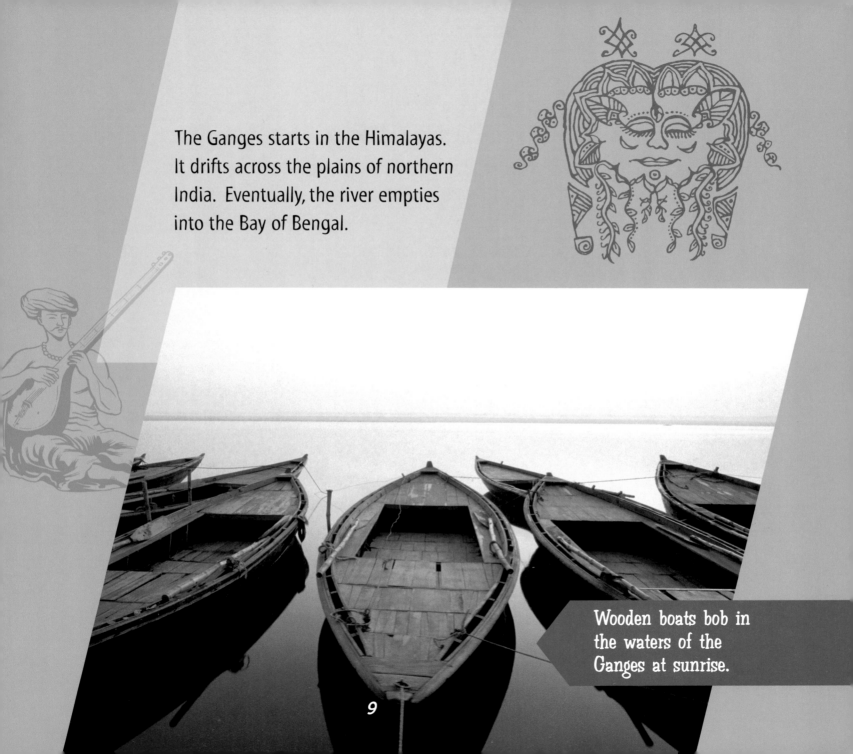

Wooden boats bob in the waters of the Ganges at sunrise.

9

First Indians

Long ago, people called the Dravidians built many towns in northern India. The Dravidians lived in brick homes. They farmed for a living. They knew how to count and how to write.

Scientists found this old city called Mohenjo Daro about seventy years ago. It was buried under layers of dirt along the Indus. The Indus is a river that runs through India and Pakistan.

Many years later, people called the Aryans took over. They pushed the Dravidians into southern India. The Aryans spoke and wrote a language called Sanskrit.

These boys come from India's oldest group of people. This group is called the Adivasi

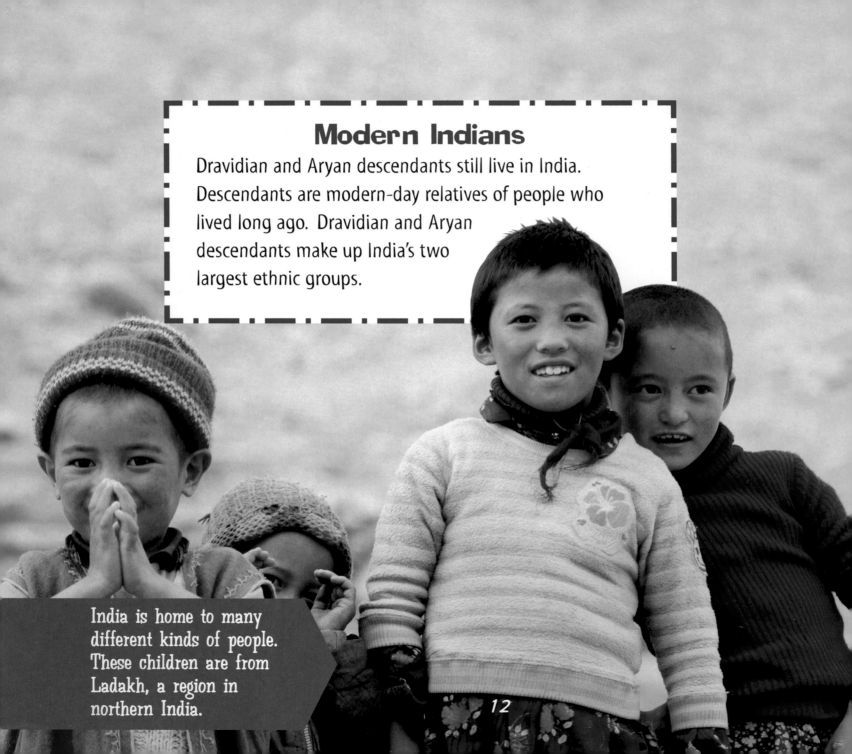

Modern Indians

Dravidian and Aryan descendants still live in India. Descendants are modern-day relatives of people who lived long ago. Dravidian and Aryan descendants make up India's two largest ethnic groups.

India is home to many different kinds of people. These children are from Ladakh, a region in northern India.

12

Dravidian descendants live in the south, just like the ancient Dravidians did. Aryan descendants live in the north. India also has many smaller ethnic groups. One group is called the Tamils. The Tamils live in the southern state of Tamil Nadu.

Meeting and Greeting in India

Indians have a special way to say hello. They bring their palms together in front of their chests, with their fingers pointing upward. Then they bow and say "namaste." *Namaste* means "I bow to thee."

This Tamil girl is dressed in brightly colored clothing.

Language

Most people in India speak English or Hindi. But the country has about sixteen other major languages.

A man in the city talks on a cell phone. What language do you think he's speaking?

14

Children in India speak many different languages.

Hindi is a common language in the north. In the south, people speak languages such as Tamil, Kannada, and Telugu.

Getting Around

How does your family get around? Many Indians use bicycles, motorbikes, and taxis. Most families don't own cars.

Riding a bike can be tricky in monsoon season! Monsoon season is a time when heavy rains fall in India.

When Indians have a long way to travel, they take a bus or a train. Buses are often packed with people. They are sometimes so crowded that passengers have to ride on the roof!

Trains are a good way to get from place to place in India.

17

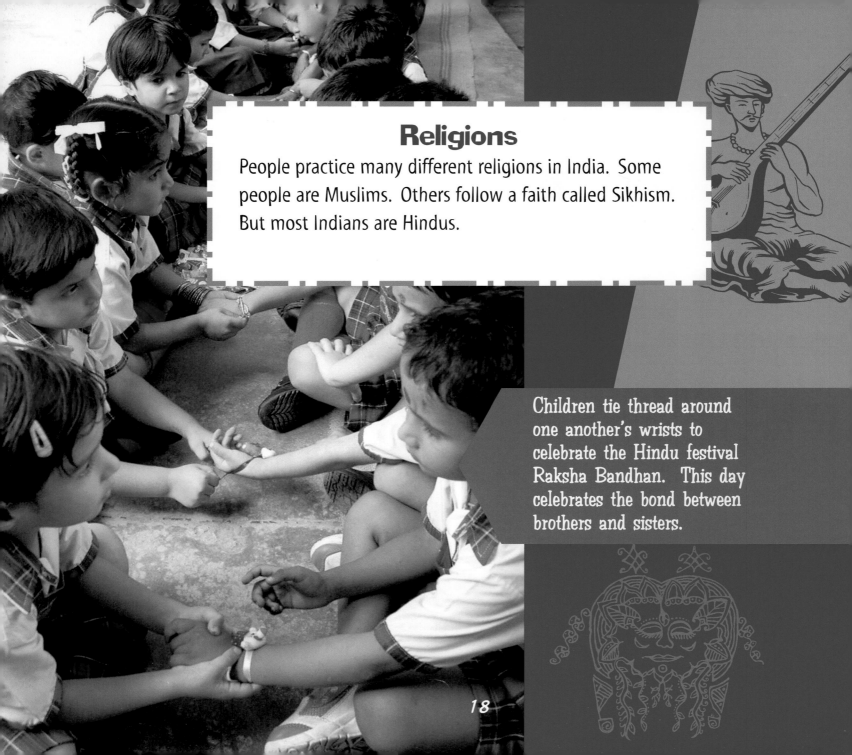

Religions

People practice many different religions in India. Some people are Muslims. Others follow a faith called Sikhism. But most Indians are Hindus.

Children tie thread around one another's wrists to celebrate the Hindu festival Raksha Bandhan. This day celebrates the bond between brothers and sisters.

18

Many Indians learn about religion when they are very young. Hindu children listen to stories from the Ramayana or the Mahabharata. These are two long, ancient Hindu books.

This carving shows the Hindu god Vishnu.

सत्यमेव जयते

Caste System

All Hindus belong to a caste. A caste is a specific social group. Some castes are wealthy and powerful. Other castes have little money or power.

This mother and daughter belong to a low caste. Members of low castes do not have the same opportunities as high-caste Indians.

Indians are born into their caste. The castes have strict rules. People from different castes cannot eat together, for example. The caste system is against the law in India. But most Hindus still follow it.

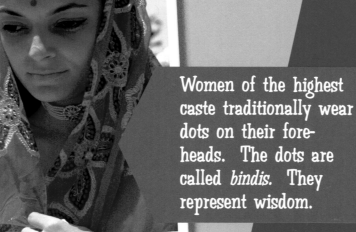

Women of the highest caste traditionally wear dots on their foreheads. The dots are called *bindis*. They represent wisdom.

Village Life

Do you live in the city or in the country? Many of India's people live in country villages. Their houses might be made of clay or brick.

These village homes are made of adobe. Adobe is a mixture of sun-dried soil and straw.

Traditional homes have open courtyards in the middle. Families eat, work, read, and talk in the courtyards. When it is hot, families might sleep in their courtyards. It's just like one big family slumber party!

Shoes Outside!

In India, it's a custom to remove your shoes before entering someone's home. Shoes are thought to be unclean because they touch dirty streets all day. If you visited a home in India, you might see neat rows of shoes and sandals sitting outside. People usually walk barefoot inside homes.

A round home sits in the state of Gujarat. Gujarat is in western India.

City Life

India's cities are jam-packed with people. Mumbai is India's biggest city. Mumbai is an island. Bridges connect it to the rest of India.

Mumbai's tall skyscrapers reach high into the sky. Mumbai used to be called Bombay.

Kolkata is another bustling Indian city. It's in the northeastern part of the country. There are lots of fun things to do in Kolkata. The city has festivals, fairs, and sporting events. But many people in Kolkata are very poor.

Two men sell vegetables outside New Market, Kolkata. Kolkata was once called Calcutta.

Two Indias

In India, the old and the new are side by side. Temples built hundreds of years ago dot the countryside. But India also has computers, freeways, and high-rise buildings.

A mother and daughter use a computer at an Internet café in Kolkata. Internet cafés have computers that people can pay to use.

Many Indians live in both worlds. At home, they might follow traditional ways. At work, they communicate with cell phones and computers.

Dear Grandpa and Grandma,

India is so much fun! Today we took a trip to Agra to see the Taj Mahal. It's a huge white building by a river. A ruler named Shah Jahan built the Taj Mahal for his favorite wife after she died. She was buried there. Did you know that twenty thousand workers built the Taj Mahal? It took them YEARS to finish the job!

See you soon!

Grandpa and Gran___
Your Town
Anywhere USA

Taj Mahal

This Indian family has four members—a mother, a father, a brother, and a sister.

Family

Whom do you live with? Kids in India often share a home with their brothers and sisters, their parents, and their grandparents. Sometimes even aunts, uncles, and cousins are part of the household.

Family Words

Here are some Hindi words for family members.

grandfather	dada	(dah-DAH)
grandmother	dadi	(dah-DEEH)
father	pita	(pi-TAAH)
mother	mata	(mah-TAAH)
uncle	chacha	(CHAH-chah)
aunt	chachi	(CHAH-cheeh)
son	beta	(bae-TAH)
daughter	beti	(BAE-teeh)
brother	bahai	(BHAA-ee)
sister	bahan	(BE-ha-nh)

सत्यमेव जयते

Many kids in India live with their grandparents.

Food

Time to eat! In India, most people eat with their fingers. Chapati is one kind of Indian food. It's a flat bread. Indians roll vegetables and a spicy sauce called curry into their chapatis.

Chapatis make a delicious Indian meal.

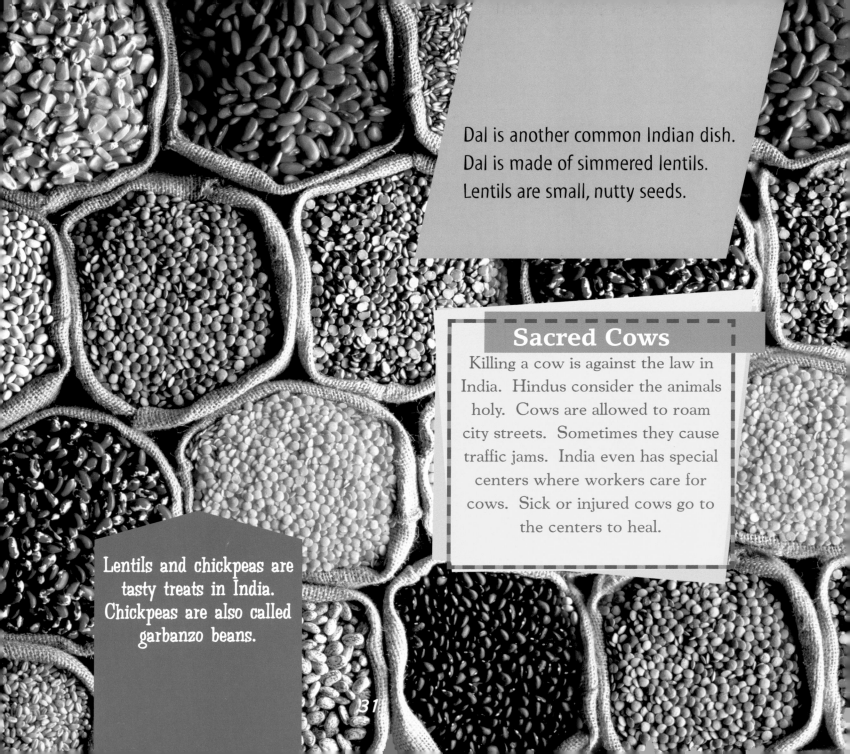

Dal is another common Indian dish. Dal is made of simmered lentils. Lentils are small, nutty seeds.

Sacred Cows

Killing a cow is against the law in India. Hindus consider the animals holy. Cows are allowed to roam city streets. Sometimes they cause traffic jams. India even has special centers where workers care for cows. Sick or injured cows go to the centers to heal.

Lentils and chickpeas are tasty treats in India. Chickpeas are also called garbanzo beans.

Clothing

Indians usually wear light, loose clothing. The clothes help keep them cool in India's hot weather. Men and boys might wear white shirts over light cotton pants. Women and girls often wear saris.

Three women wear traditional clothing on a lunch break in Bangalore. Their meal probably looks very familiar to you!

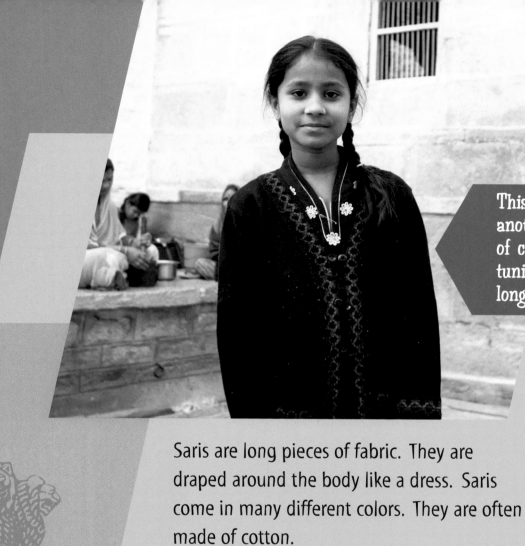

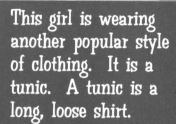

This girl is wearing another popular style of clothing. It is a tunic. A tunic is a long, loose shirt.

Saris are long pieces of fabric. They are draped around the body like a dress. Saris come in many different colors. They are often made of cotton.

सत्यमेव जयते

School Days

Kids in India start school when they are six years old. But not every child in India goes to school. More boys than girls attend classes. Girls from small villages sometimes stay home to help their mothers.

Some children in India go to school. But others work at home or take on jobs to help their families.

Children make watercolor handprints at this Indian school.

Kids learn about math, history, and geography. Many students also study English or Hindi. Others study their local languages.

Women spread colored powder on one another's faces to celebrate Holi.

Holidays

Once a year, the people of India celebrate Children's Day. Parents hold small parties for their kids. Holi is an important Hindu festival. It marks the coming of spring. During Holi, people chase their friends around and shower them with colored powder!

36

Diwali takes place in the fall. Diwali is the Hindu festival of lights. Families clean their homes, light oil lamps, trade candy, and set off fireworks.

Body Painting

Indians have a special way to celebrate weddings and other important events. They practice *mehndi*, the art of body painting. Mehndi designs look a little like tattoos. The designs are very fancy. They often decorate the hands and feet of brides in India.

Oil lamps are an important part of Diwali celebrations.

Both young and old enjoy cricket in India.

Cricket Time

Indians love cricket. And we are not talking about a bug! Cricket is a little like baseball—but *only* a little.

Two teams of eleven players play a cricket match. One team bats while the other team fields. Players hit the ball and run between two bases called wickets. If the batter hits the ball and a fielder catches it, then the batter is out. After ten outs, the teams switch places.

Have you ever watched a game of cricket?

39

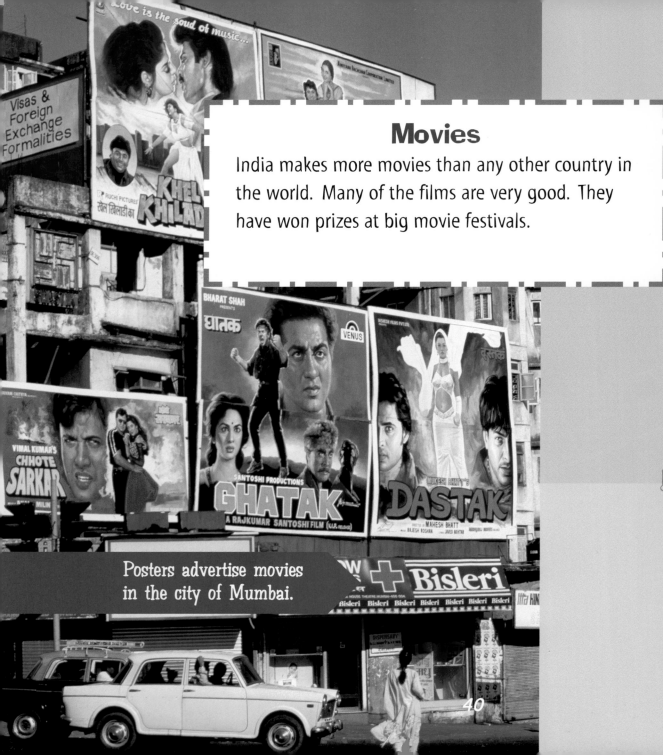

Movies

India makes more movies than any other country in the world. Many of the films are very good. They have won prizes at big movie festivals.

Posters advertise movies in the city of Mumbai.

All Indian movies have action, romance, and comedy. Good guys fight bad guys, and the good guys always win. Actors often sing and dance to show what is going on.

Movie fans watch a film at a theater in India.

Music

Two instruments are popular in India. They are called the sitar and the *tanpoura*. The sitar has strings. It looks a little bit like a guitar. The tanpoura is another stringed instrument. Tanpoura players strum a single note, over and over again.

The sitar is a traditional Indian instrument. It has strings and a very long neck.

Folk music is popular in India too. This music is played during celebrations. Many Indians also listen to pop songs and music from Indian films.

Ravi Shankar is a popular Indian musician. He is playing the sitar with his daughter Anoushka.

THE FLAG OF INDIA

India's flag is orange, white, and green. The orange stripe stands for sacrifice and courage. The white stripe stands for truth. The green stripe stands for soil and plant life. It represents Indians' relationship with the land. A blue wheel sits in the middle of the flag. The wheel is an ancient symbol. It stands for the cycles of life and fate.

FAST FACTS

FULL COUNTRY NAME: Republic of India

AREA: 1,269,340 square miles (3,287,590 square kilometers), or slightly more than one-third the size of the United States

MAIN LANDFORMS: the mountain range the Himalayas; the Indo-Gangetic Plain; the Deccan Plateau

MAJOR RIVERS: Ganges, Indus, Brahmaputra, Narmada, Mahanadi, Godavari, Krishna, Cauvery

ANIMALS AND THEIR HABITATS: tigers (forest), elephants (forests and grasslands), peacocks (forests and shallow streams), Indian cobras (forest)

CAPITAL CITY: New Delhi

OFFICIAL LANGUAGES: Hindi is the national language, but the country has about sixteen other major languages.

POPULATION: about 1,129,866,154

GLOSSARY

caste: a specific social group. People in castes hold traditional places and jobs in Indian culture.

chapati: a flat bread made from whole wheat flour and cooked on a griddle

continent: any one of seven large areas of land. The continents are Africa, Antarctica, Asia, Australia, Europe, North America, and South America.

courtyard: an open area similar to a backyard

dal: a dish made of small, nutty seeds called lentils

descendant: a modern-day relative of people who lived long ago

ethnic group: a large community of people that shares the same language, religion, and customs

map: a drawing or chart of all or part of Earth or the sky

mountain: a part of Earth's surface that rises high into the sky

plain: a large area of flat land

religion: a system of belief and worship

sari: a long piece of fabric that is draped around the body like a dress

temple: a religious place where people go to worship

TO LEARN MORE

BOOKS

Arnold, Caroline, and Madeleine Comora. *Taj Mahal*. Minneapolis: Carolrhoda Books, 2007. This book tells the love story behind the building of the Taj Mahal. It also provides interesting information on Indian culture.

Italia, Bob. *India*. Edina, MN: Abdo, 2002. Learn more about the people and places of India in this title.

Petersen, David. *Asia*. New York: Children's Press, 1998. Read all about Asia—the continent on which India lies.

Zucker, Jonny. *Lighting a Lamp: A Diwali Story*. Hauppauge, NY: Barrons, 2004. Follow along as a family exchanges sweets, lights candles, and watches fireworks to celebrate the Hindu festival Diwali.

WEBSITES

India
https://www.cia.gov/library/publications/the-world-factbook/geos/in.html
This website features many useful facts about India.

Mughal India
http://www.mughalindia.co.uk/room.html
On this interactive site from the British Museum, you can learn what India was like under Mughal (Muslim) rule in the sixteenth and seventeenth centuries.

INDEX

The photographs in this book are used with the permission of: © Steve Vidler/SuperStock, pp. 4, 27; © age fotostock/SuperStock, pp. 6, 19, 24, 30; © Photononstop/SuperStock, p. 7; © Michele Burgess/SuperStock, p. 8; © Pacific Stock/SuperStock, p. 9; © Yoshio Tomii/SuperStock, p. 10; © Dinodia Photo Library, pp. 11, 15, 17, 28, 29, 34, 35, 37 (both), 42; © Sherab/Alamy, p. 12; © SuperStock, Inc./SuperStock, p. 13; © Dinodia Images/Alamy, p. 14; © Harish Tyagi/epa/Corbis, p. 16; © Narinder Nanu/Stringer/AFP/Getty Images, p. 18; © Sajjad Hussain/Stringer/AFP/Getty Images, p. 20; © Charles & Josette Lenars/CORBIS, p. 21; © Michael Freeman/CORBIS, p. 22; © Robert Harding Picture Library Ltd/Alamy, p. 23; © Richard I'Anson/Lonely Planet Images/Getty Images, p. 25; © Jayanta Shaw/Reuters/Corbis, p. 26; © Thomas Del Brase/Stone/Getty Images, p. 31; © Fredrik Renander/Alamy, p. 32; © Renaud Visage/Photographer's Choice/Getty Images, p. 33; © epa/Corbis, p. 36; © Richard Powers/CORBIS, p. 38; © Arko Datta/Reuters/Corbis, p. 39; © Catherine Karnow/CORBIS, p. 40; © Noshir Desai/Corbis, p. 41; © John Van Hasselt/Corbis, p. 43.
Illustrations by © Bill Hauser/Independent Picture Service

Cover: © Dinodia Photo Library